On the banks of this river lived a greedy crocodile.

His name was Crunch.

All the creatures of the river would tremble when they heard his voice,

"Crunch and munch!
Crunch and munch!
My name is Crunch,
And I want my lunch!"

When the fish heard him coming,
they would swim away.

When the frogs heard him coming,
they would hop away.

When the worms heard him coming,
they would wriggle away.

When the snakes heard him coming,
they would slither away.

And when the lizards heard him coming,
they would *run!*

One morning, very early, before the sun
brought warmth to the damp river air,
the creatures held a secret meeting.

Crunch had made them all afraid.

"*We're* too small to fight him," said a fish. "That's why we swim away."

"He is too big for all of *us*," said one of the frogs.

"He creeps up on *us* when we sit on our nests," said a bird sadly.

"He squashes *us* into the mud with his feet,"
said a worm.

"He snaps at *us* when we lie on the rocks
to warm ourselves in the sun,"
said a lizard and a snake together.

The creatures plotted and planned.
The first rays of light were touching the trees
when they quietly went back to their homes.

It wasn't long before they heard a familiar
sound . . .

"Crunch and munch!
Crunch and munch!
My name is Crunch
and I *want* my lunch!"

How they hated that sound!

But today, they had been waiting for it.
Today, they had a plan!

As Crunch came creeping and searching
and snapping his great toothy jaws . . .

The fish swam towards him.
The frogs hopped towards him.
The birds flew towards him.
The worms wriggled towards him.
The snakes slithered towards him.
And the lizards *ran!*

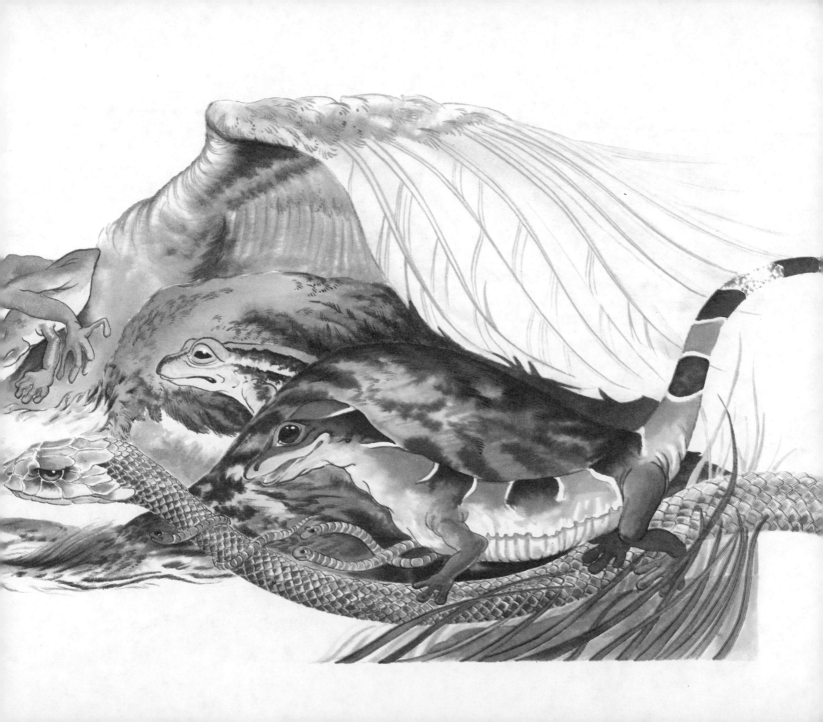

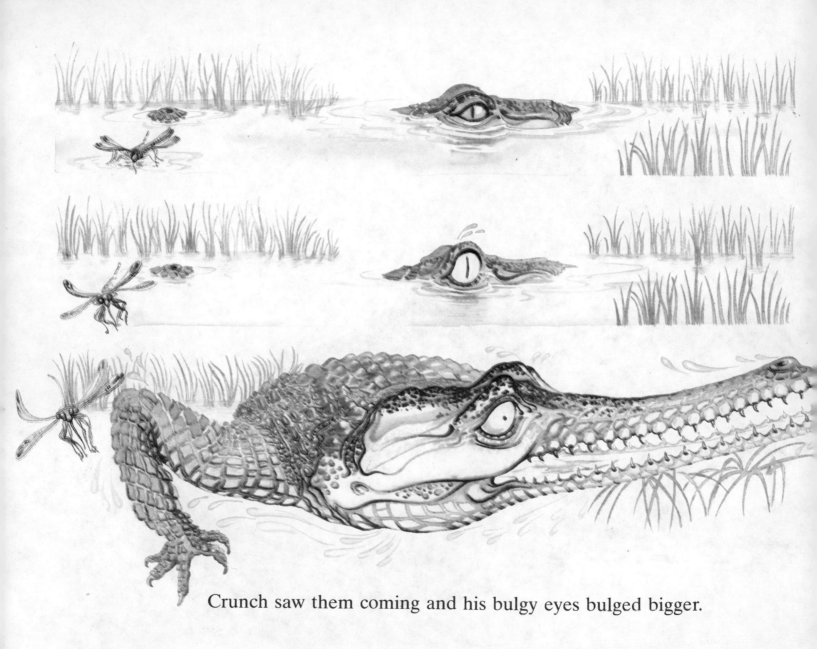

Crunch saw them coming and his bulgy eyes bulged bigger.

The fish were chasing *him!*
The frogs were chasing *him!*
The birds and lizards and snakes and worms
were all coming nearer and *nearer!*

What a big,
gigantic *monstrous* meal
Crunch could have.
All he had to do was
open his mouth
and let them come in.

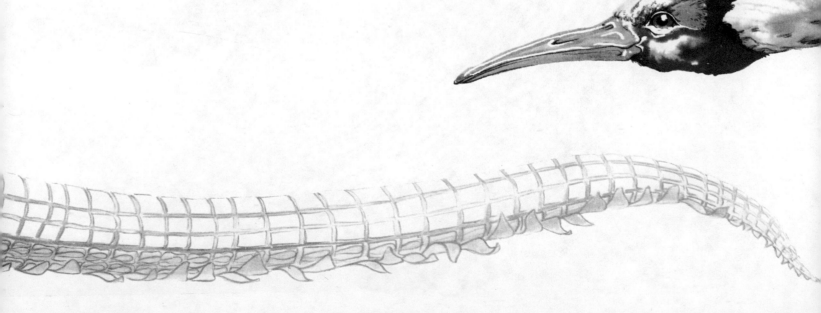

But Crunch was not only greedy.
He was also a terrible coward.

He could hear the lizards' feet tapping as they ran,
the birds' wings flapping as they flew,
and the fishes' tails swishing as they swam.
All the creatures *stared* at Crunch
as they came closer and *closer*.

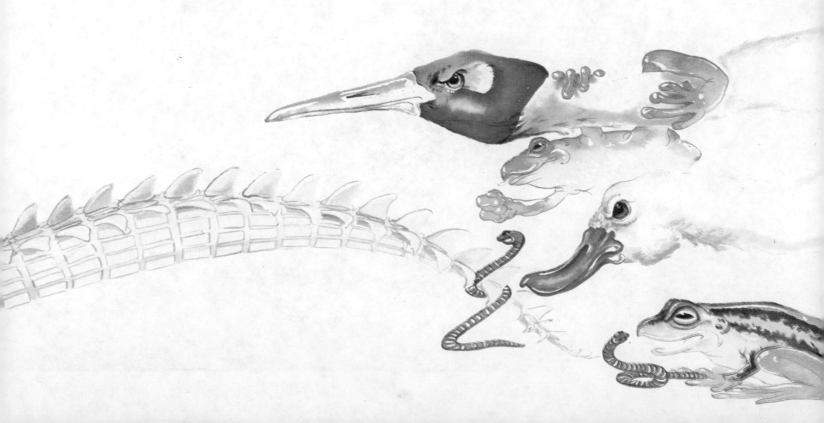

Crunch turned.

Crunch ran.

He slipped in the mud
and splashed in the water
as he hurried and scurried away.

Crunch kept going. He didn't want any
swimming, running, hopping, wriggling,
or flapping things coming after *him*!

The creatures of the river stopped and listened.

Crunch kept on running.

The birds twittered, the frogs croaked,
and the worms glugged in the mud.

Then the creatures turned from the chase.
The fish swam,
the frogs hopped,
the birds flew,
the worms wriggled,
the snakes slithered,
and the lizards stood up and *ran*
home to their own part of the river.

By evening the river was peaceful again.
When the shadows of the trees
were long and dark upon the water and
wind was sweeping ripples through the reeds,
the creatures of the river fell asleep.

For Joelie

ISBN 0-590-41050-4

Text copyright © 1986 by Josephine Croser.
Illustrations copyright © 1986 by Carol McLean-Carr.
All rights reserved. This edition published by Scholastic Inc.,
730 Broadway, New York, NY 10003, by arrangement with Ashton Scholastic Pty. Limited.

12 11 10 9 8 7 6 5 4 3 2 1   7 8 9/8 0 1 2/9

Printed in the U.S.A.   09

First Scholastic printing, April 1987